By the Light of the Moon

For my good friends, Sharon and Ian
~ S. C.
For you, Pa, with love
~ G. H.

This edition published by Scholastic Inc; 557 Broadway; New York, NY 10012,
by arrangement with Little Tiger Press. SCHOLASTIC and associated logos
are trademarks and/or registered trademarks of Scholastic Inc
Scholastic Canada; Markham, Ontario

International Standard Book Number: 1-84506-434-8

Text copyright © Sheridan Cain 2006
Illustrations copyright © Gaby Hansen 2006

Original edition published in English by Little Tiger Press,
an imprint of Magi Publications, London, England, 2005.

This edition originally published by Tiger Tales, an imprint of ME Media, LLC,
202 Old Ridgefield Road, Wilton, CT 06897

Library of Congress Cataloging-in-Publication Data is available for this title.

Printed in China

By the Light of the Moon

Sheridan Cain   Gaby Hansen

tiger tales

The moon shone bright in the evening sky as Mother Mouse watched over Little Mouse. He lay curled and snuggly tight, a grassy nook for his bed. High above, a starry blanket twinkled silver.

"Sleep tight, Little Mouse," she whispered.

But just then, Mole tumbled through the grass.

"Mother Mouse," he said, "you can't leave your baby there. The farmer is coming to plow the field. That bed is not safe."

"Oh dear!" said Mother Mouse, hugging Little Mouse close. "Where can my Little Mouse sleep?"

"His bed should be underground," said Mole. "That's where Little Mouse could sleep."

So Mother
Mouse scritched
and scratched
the soft earth.

Soon the hole was
deep, and she tucked
Little Mouse into his
new bed.

Little Mouse snuggled down, but he could not fall asleep. There was no moon.

"Mommy!" he cried. "It's so dark. I can't sleep."

Owl, watching from the willow tree, heard Little Mouse cry.

"Mother Mouse," he said, "that bed is much too dark for Little Mouse."

"Oh my!" said Mother Mouse. "Where can my Little Mouse sleep?"

"Where the moon is brighter," said Owl. "Up there in the tree is where Little Mouse could sleep."

Mother Mouse spotted an empty nest, and she placed Little Mouse in his new bed. Little Mouse snuggled down, but the wind was strong and his bed felt wobbly.

"Mommy!" he cried. "I'm dizzy! It's very high up here. I might fall out."

Little Mouse's cry
woke Duck.

"Mother Mouse," she
called, "that bed is much
too high for Little Mouse."

"Oh no!" said Mother
Mouse. "Where can my
Little Mouse sleep?"

"A bed of reeds would
be cozy," said Duck.
"That's where Little Mouse
could sleep."

So Mother Mouse carried Little Mouse to the river's edge.

She hopped and jumped and flattened the reedy leaves...

and placed Little Mouse in his new bed. Little Mouse snuggled down, but soon he felt cold.

"Mommy!" he cried. "I don't like this squishy squashy bed. It's damp. I might sink."

Mother Mouse carried Little Mouse back to the riverbank. Hugging him tightly, she hung her head and sighed. "Where, oh where, can my Little Mouse sleep?"

She looked
into Little Mouse's eyes.
They sparkled in the soft
light of the moon. Mother
Mouse looked up at the
moon, and the moon
winked back at her.
Mother Mouse smiled.

She thought back to when she was
small. She remembered her mother's
bright eyes watching over her. She
remembered her blanket of silver stars.
And she remembered the
soft light of the moon
shining above her.

Mother Mouse looked toward the field that had been her home since she was tiny. Her eyes sparkled. The farmer had plowed—but in the shelter of the big tree her home stood safe!

Mother Mouse carried
Little Mouse back to his old
bed. She gently tucked him
in, and Little Mouse
snuggled tight.

"Mommy," he said,
yawning. "This is my bed,
and it is just right."

"Of course it is," said
Mother Mouse. "Sleep tight,
Little Mouse."